Copyright © 1985 by Karen Erickson and Maureen Roffey. All rights reserved. Produced for the publishers by Sadie Fields Productions Ltd, London. First published in the United States by Scholastic Inc.

12 11 10 9 8 7 6 5 4 3 2 1   2   5 6 7 8 9 / 8

Printed and bound by
L.E.G.O., Vicenza, Italy

I Can Settle Down

Karen Erickson and Maureen Roffey

Scholastic Inc.

New York Toronto London Auckland Sydney Tokyo

Everything is so exciting.
I can't calm down.

My legs keep jumping.
My arms keep moving.
My mouth makes loud sounds.

Wait a minute.
Maybe I can settle down.
Maybe.

First, I sit down. Close my eyes.

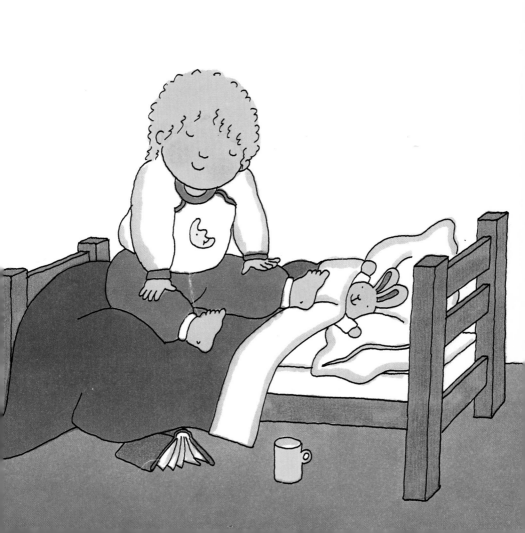

Oops! There goes my
busy body again.
I'm standing on my hands.

I'll try again. I sit down.
Close my eyes. Pretend I'm
floating in a quiet pond.

Breathe in and out.
In and out.

Shhhh.
Listen to my breath.
Listen to the sounds in
the room.
Listen to the sounds outside.

Look at my tummy going up
and down.
Breathe in-out. In-out. In-out.

I'm not moving.
My arms drop. My hands
dangle. My feet are still.

I curl up under my soft,
fluffy blanket.

Look. I settled down.
I can do it!
I did it!